Susie's Bad Day Blues

Arjun Chatterjee
Art by Paula Becker

GRAPHIC READERS

Literacy Consultants
David Booth • Larry Swartz

Ru^{bicon} www.rubiconpublishing.com

Editorial Director: Amy Land
Project Editor: Dawna McKinnon
Creative Director: Jennifer Drew
Art Director: Rebecca Buchanan

Printed in Singapore

ISBN: 978-1-77058-562-1
3 4 5 6 7 8 9 10 11 12 2016   25 24 23 22 21 20 19 18 17 16
4500568939

Can Susie find the cure for the Bad Day Blues?

CHARACTERS

Susie

Ms. Rogers

Traveling Sam

Susie's Sister

Becks

Madison

Susie woke up grumpy. She stumbled out of bed and stubbed her big toe.

Owww!

She quickly got dressed. There were only two socks left in her drawer, and they were different colors.

Susie poured cereal for breakfast... but there was no milk.

3

It was a hot day, but Susie wore her big rubber boots to hide her mismatched socks.

Why is Susie wearing those big rubber boots?

Don't mind her. She's got the Bad Day Blues!

Susie spotted a big puddle...

Hey, guys! Check out what I can do!

In the classroom...

I hope no one makes fun of my boots.

Hi, Susie. Why are you wearing boots?

Susie turned to her best friend, Becks.

I probably shouldn't sit next to you, Becks. I've got a BAD case of the Bad Day Blues.

Stay away from Susie! My mom says bad days are like colds — you can catch them!

Ouch!

Bump!

See, I told you! Now Jimmy has the Bad Day Blues, too!

The Bad Day Blues were rubbing off on everyone on the playground.

Comprehension Strategy:
Making Inferences

Common Core Reading Standards

Foundational Skills

3a. Distinguish long and short vowels when reading regularly spelled one-syllable words.

3f. Recognize and read grade-appropriate irregularly spelled words.

Literature

4. Describe how words and phrases (e.g., regular beats, alliteration, rhymes, repeated lines) supply rhythm and meaning in a story.

7. Use information gained from the illustrations and words in a print or digital text to demonstrate understanding.

Reading Foundations

Word Study: Compound Words

High-Frequency Words: boot, catch, class, different, everyone, friend, gave, hope, laugh, left, lunch, really, stay, thought

Reading Vocabulary: classroom, cure, grumpy, indoor, lunchtime, office, playground, recess, remember, worry

Fluency: Conveying Emotion and Meaning

BEFORE Reading

Prereading Strategy ▶ Activating Prior Knowledge

- Point to the title and read it aloud. Then point to the picture on the cover. Say: *Being caught in the rain without an umbrella would be a bad day. Have you ever had a bad day? Share something you already know about bad days.*

Introduce the Comprehension Strategy

- Point to the Making Inferences visual on the inside front cover of this book. Say: *Now we're going to practice making inferences. When you make an inference, you figure out something the author doesn't explain by using what you already know and by looking for clues in the story. Let's try it.*

- Point to the bottom picture on page 5. Draw a three-column chart on the board. From left to right, label the columns *Clues, What I Know,* and *My Inference*.

  Modeling Example Say: *I see clues that tell me why Susie is so upset. Susie has jumped in a puddle, and there was a hole in her boot. I'll write these clues in the* Clues *column. I know that puddles are full of water. A boot with a hole is not waterproof. I also know having wet feet is not fun. I'll write "not waterproof," "wet," and "not fun" under* What I Know. *Even though the text doesn't say it, I infer that Susie is upset because her foot got wet. I'll write my inference on the board.*

- Say: *Good readers make inferences because it helps us understand what we read. Making inferences helps us to find what the author does not explain.*